From Streets to Stardust : A Blaxploitation Strip-Lit Romance

James Daniel

Published by James Daniel, 2024.

This is a work of fiction. Similarities to real people, places, or events are entirely coincidental.

FROM STREETS TO STARDUST : A BLAXPLOITATION STRIP-LIT ROMANCE

First edition. June 16, 2024.

ISBN: 979-8230034629

Written by James Daniel.

Chapter 1 - The Streets That Raised Her

BETTY'S JOURNEY BEGAN amidst the concrete maze of a bustling urban sprawl, where the heartbeat of the city pulsed with soulful melodies and the promise of sultry nights.

Raised by her indomitable grandmother in the shadows of towering high-rises and neon-lit alleys, Betty learned early on that survival meant more than just navigating the streets — it meant thriving despite the odds stacked against her

Her physical presence mirrored the resilience forged in the crucible of her upbringing. With jet-black hair coiled into an untamed afro and a complexion kissed by the sun, Betty moved through the world with an aura that blended defiance and grace. Her eyes, a deep, mysterious brown, mirrored the depths of her ambitions—a reflection of a soul undaunted by the challenges of her environment

From a young age, Betty found solace and inspiration in the rhythmic beats of soul music that echoed through the community. It was in these melodies that she discovered her own voice, often performing at local clubs where the air hummed with both opportunity and danger. Yet, beneath her bold exterior lay a heart of gold, fiercely protective of her grandmother and deeply loyal to the few friends who earned her trust.

As she matured, Betty's dreams expanded beyond the concrete jungle that raised her. She harbored a passion for fashion, sketching designs that blended retro chic with a modern flair—a testament to her innate creativity and determination to transcend her humble beginnings. Each stroke of her pencil on paper whispered of aspirations far grander than the city's boundaries could contain

But Betty's path was not without obstacles. The streets taught her early on the bitter taste of betrayal and the precariousness of independence. Her parents' absence loomed as a void, their distant figures casting a long shadow over her formative years. Yet, where others saw abandonment, Betty found strength in the unwavering support of her grandmother—a beacon of love and wisdom in a world where trust came at a premium

As she navigated the urban landscape, Betty's encounters often intertwined with Terry, a figure whose imposing presence belied a complexity that intrigued her. His salt-and-pepper hair and piercing blue eyes held stories of their own, tales of a life marked by struggle and a quest for redemption. Terry's journey, woven with hers through chance meetings and shared moments, hinted at a connection deeper than the city's surface allure.

In the heart of this urban labyrinth, Betty danced on the edge of discovery, her spirit unyielding against the backdrop of a city that both fueled her ambitions and tested her resolve. Her story, etched against the backdrop of glitz and glamour under neon lights, was a testament to the allure of fame and the price of success—a journey fueled by passion, desire, and an unwavering belief in the power of dreams.

In the vibrant tapestry of the city's heartbeat, Betty's presence resonated like a soulful melody—a blend of defiance and grace that set her apart in the bustling urban landscape. Her story began in the heart of a neighborhood where concrete walls echoed with the dreams of those who dared to defy their circumstances

Betty, with her jet-black hair framing a face that mirrored both strength and vulnerability, moved through life with a rhythm that matched the pulsating beat of soul music. Her eyes, a deep, mysterious brown, held the wisdom of someone who had weathered storms far beyond her years. From the tender age when she first felt the rhythm of the city coursing through her veins, Betty knew she was destined for more than the streets could offer.

Raised by her grandmother—a pillar of resilience in a world where adversity was a constant companion—Betty found solace in the vivid hues of her sketches and the soul-stirring notes of jazz that filled their modest home. Her grandmother's love and guidance provided a steady anchor amidst the tempest of uncertainty, instilling in Betty a belief in her own potential and a passion for fashion that bloomed like a rare orchid in the urban jungle.

Her aspirations soared beyond the confines of her neighborhood, reaching for the stars that glittered above the skyline. Betty's dreams were not mere fantasies; they were the lifeline she clung to amidst the challenges that threatened to overshadow her path. Dancing in smoky clubs to earn a living, she wove threads of hope into every step, her movements a testament to resilience forged in the crucible of adversity.

But beneath Betty's bold exterior lay a tender heart, fiercely protective of her grandmother and loyal to the few friends who understood the rhythm of her soul. Her fear of betrayal and losing her hard-won independence loomed large, a shadow cast by the absence of her parents—a void she filled with determination and an unyielding spirit.

In the midst of this urban symphony, Betty's encounters with Terry, a figure with a past etched in the weathered lines of his face, added layers of intrigue to her narrative. His presence, both enigmatic and reassuring, hinted at a shared journey through the labyrinthine streets and into the uncharted territories of the heart. Their paths, intertwined by fate's hand, spoke of a connection deeper than the neon-lit glamour that adorned the city's surface.

As Betty's story unfolded against the backdrop of glittering penthouses and dimly lit jazz clubs, she stood at the precipice of discovery—a dreamer's heartbeat echoing through the concrete jungle, each pulse a testament to her unwavering belief in the power of dreams. Her journey, marked by passion, desire, and the relentless pursuit of a future carved by her own hands, beckoned to those who dared to listen to the whispers of possibility amidst the cacophony of the city's streets.

The decision to move to the city was a crescendo in Betty's symphony of aspirations—a bold stroke on the canvas of her life, painted with hues of hope and the promise of opportunity. Leaving behind the familiar embrace of her grandmother's home, she ventured into the heart of the urban jungle where dreams were forged and destinies rewritten under the watchful glow of neon lights.

The city greeted Betty with open arms and a cacophony of sounds—the hustle and bustle of daily life intertwining with the soulful melodies that had shaped her spirit since childhood. Amidst the towering skyscrapers and bustling streets, she found herself navigating a labyrinth of possibilities, each corner promising a chance encounter that could alter the course of her journey.

Her new apartment, a modest sanctuary amidst the urban sprawl, became a canvas for her dreams. With walls adorned by sketches of haute couture designs and windows framing a skyline that whispered of endless potential, Betty embraced her newfound independence with a mixture of apprehension and determination. The city's pulse beat in harmony with her own, urging her to seize opportunities with both hands and weave them into the fabric of her ambitions.

Yet, amidst the glittering facade of penthouses and designer boutiques, Betty encountered the harsh realities of city life. The competitive world of fashion, where trends shifted like sand dunes in a desert storm, posed challenges that tested her resilience and creativity. Undeterred by setbacks and fueled by a passion that burned brighter than the city lights, she poured her soul into each design, infusing them with a blend of retro chic and contemporary flair that spoke of her unique vision.

Her journey was not without its companions. Terry's presence continued to weave through the tapestry of her days, his weathered hands guiding her through the pitfalls of urban existence with a quiet strength that mirrored her own determination. Their friendship blossomed amidst late-night jazz sessions and impromptu walks through the city's hidden corners, each moment deepening the connection that bound their fates together.

As Betty navigated the ebb and flow of city life, she discovered allies in unexpected places—fellow dreamers who shared her passion for breaking boundaries and challenging conventions. Together, they formed a tapestry of support and camaraderie, their shared aspirations creating a mosaic of hope amidst the concrete jungle's relentless pace.

Through it all, Betty remained steadfast in her belief that dreams were meant to be chased, not merely chased after. Her journey, illuminated by the flickering lights of ambition and fueled by the rhythm of her heart, echoed through the city streets—a testament to the courage of those who dared to dance to their own urban melodies.

In the heart of the urban jungle, Betty's journey intertwined with the vibrant tapestry of blaxploitation and strip-lit romance—a homage to the rich cultural tapestry that shaped her dreams and aspirations. As she immersed herself deeper into the pulsating rhythms of the city, Betty found herself drawn to worlds where passion and desire intertwined with ambition, mirroring her own quest for recognition and belonging.

The influence of blaxploitation culture, with its bold narratives and larger-than-life protagonists, resonated deeply with Betty's own journey from humble beginnings to the brink of stardom. Inspired by iconic figures who defied conventions and carved their own paths through adversity, she channeled their spirit into her designs and performances, infusing them with a sense of empowerment and authenticity that spoke to her roots.

Strip-lit romance, with its provocative blend of sensuality and emotional depth, provided a canvas for Betty to explore the complexities of love and desire against the backdrop of a city that never slept. Her encounters with Terry, whose presence in her life grew more profound with each passing day, echoed the passionate dynamics of protagonists who navigated the blurred lines between attraction and vulnerability.

Through her sketches and performances, Betty paid homage to the soulful melodies that had shaped her identity—a tribute to the music that echoed through the city's streets and the voices that sang of struggle and triumph. Each design became a testament to her journey, weaving threads of retro chic with modern flair to create garments that whispered of resilience and ambition.

As she delved deeper into the world of fashion and entertainment, Betty found herself at the intersection of glamour and grit—a place where dreams collided with harsh realities, and success demanded sacrifices she had never imagined. The allure of fame beckoned, its tantalizing promises tempered by the price of success—a price Betty was willing to pay, armed with nothing but her talent and unwavering determination.

In the midst of this cultural renaissance, Betty's evolution from dreamer to doer unfolded like a chapter from a strip-lit romance, each page turning with anticipation and apprehension. Her journey, marked by passion and driven by a hunger for recognition, resonated with those who dared to defy expectations and rewrite their own narratives amidst the glitz and glamor of the city's skyline.

As the city's soulful rhythms echoed through her veins, Betty stood poised on the threshold of greatness—a testament to the power of dreams nurtured in the heart of a concrete jungle where every heartbeat carried the promise of possibility.

Betty's immersion into the soul movement was a tapestry woven with threads of cultural resonance, each strand reflecting the vibrant hues of her journey through the urban landscape. As she navigated the pulsating rhythms of the city, she discovered a deeper connection to her roots—a resonance that transcended mere fashion and performance, echoing the soulful melodies that had shaped her identity from the very beginning.

In the heart of the city's bustling nightlife, Betty found herself drawn to venues where soul music reverberated through dimly lit halls, evoking emotions as raw and powerful as the voices that filled the air. It was here, amidst the clinking of glasses and the sway of bodies lost in rhythm, that Betty felt most alive—a testament to the transformative power of music in her life.

Her designs, now infused with the spirit of the soul movement, became a canvas for storytelling—a tribute to the icons who had paved the way with their voices and their courage. Each garment spoke of resilience and pride, blending retro chic with modern sensibilities to create a narrative that celebrated both the past and the future of African American culture.

But Betty's journey was not confined to the stage or the runway. As she immersed herself deeper into the soul movement, she found herself confronting issues of identity and representation within the fashion industry—a landscape where diversity was often overlooked in favor of mainstream trends. Armed with her talent and a fierce determination to challenge conventions, Betty became a voice for change, advocating for inclusivity and authenticity in an industry hungry for innovation.

Her partnership with Terry, whose own journey mirrored hers in its quest for redemption and acceptance, blossomed amidst the backdrop of cultural resurgence. Together, they navigated the complexities of love and ambition, their bond deepening with each shared triumph and setback. Terry's unwavering support became a cornerstone in Betty's evolution, his presence a testament to the power of solidarity in a world where success often came at a steep price.

As Betty's star rose within the soul movement, so too did her influence as a trailblazer and a voice for change. Her journey, etched against the backdrop of glitz and glamor under neon lights, resonated with those who saw in her a reflection of their own struggles and aspirations. Through her designs and performances, Betty became a beacon of hope and possibility—a testament to the enduring power of resilience and the transformative impact of embracing one's cultural heritage.

In the soulful rhythms that echoed through her veins, Betty discovered not only a platform for self-expression but also a community of like-minded souls who shared her passion for authenticity and inclusivity. Together, they forged a path forward, their footsteps echoing through the city streets—a testament to the enduring legacy of the soul movement and the indomitable spirit of those who dared to dream.

Betty's journey through the urban labyrinth was guided by the steady heartbeat of her grandmother's wisdom—a melody that resonated through every note of her life's symphony. Raised in the embrace of a woman whose strength defied the challenges of their gritty neighborhood, Betty found solace and inspiration in the unwavering love and guidance that shaped her into the woman she was becoming.

Her grandmother's presence was a sanctuary amidst the chaos of the city—a haven where Betty's dreams found fertile ground to bloom. With each sketch that adorned their modest home and each performance that echoed through local clubs, Betty carried with her the echoes of her grandmother's voice, a reminder of the resilience and grace that defined their shared journey.

From a young age, Betty learned the art of survival from the woman who had weathered life's storms with dignity and courage. Her grandmother's stories of resilience and triumph became the foundation upon which Betty built her own aspirations, instilling in her a belief in the power of perseverance and the importance of staying true to oneself in the face of adversity.

As Betty ventured deeper into the world of fashion and entertainment, her grandmother's lessons continued to resonate—a quiet strength that bolstered her spirit and fortified her resolve. Through the ups and downs of her journey, Betty found herself drawing upon the wisdom imparted by her grandmother, whose unwavering faith in her abilities became a guiding light in moments of doubt and uncertainty.

Their bond, forged through years of shared laughter and tears, transcended the confines of their modest home and permeated every facet of Betty's evolving identity. Her grandmother's presence loomed large in every decision, every sketch, and every performance—a testament to the enduring power of familial love and the transformative impact of a guiding hand.

As Betty embraced the soul movement and carved out her place in the city's cultural landscape, she carried with her the legacy of her grandmother's teachings—a legacy woven into the fabric of her dreams and aspirations. Through her successes and setbacks, Betty remained rooted in the values instilled by her grandmother, whose wisdom resonated in every note of the soulful melodies that shaped her journey.

In the city's bustling streets and glittering venues, Betty's grandmother's spirit remained a constant presence—a source of strength and inspiration that propelled her forward in pursuit of her dreams. Theirs was a bond forged in love and fortified by shared experiences—a testament to the enduring influence of those who believed in her unconditionally.

Betty moved through the city like a panther prowling its territory. The streets were her stage, the rhythm of life pulsating through her veins like the bassline of a soulful melody. Her ambition burned brighter than the neon lights that adorned the clubs where she performed. From the humble beginnings of her grandmother's worn-down apartment in the heart of the city's toughest neighborhood, Betty had dreamed of stardom.

Her journey was etched with the grit of survival and the shimmer of ambition. Raised by her wise and loving grandmother, she learned early on that life's stage could be as treacherous as it was promising. Betty's physical presence, with her jet-black afro and eyes that held the mysteries of a thousand stories, commanded attention. Yet, it was her voice—a blend of honey and fire—that captivated audiences, weaving tales of heartache and triumph.

In this urban jungle where every shadow seemed to whisper secrets, Betty's rise was a testament to resilience. She had been a waitress by day and a soulful songstress by night, pouring her heart into every note sung at smoky clubs where dreams mingled with cigarette smoke. Terry, the weathered saxophonist with a past as storied as the city itself, recognized Betty's talent like a gem hidden in plain sight.

Their encounters were more than chance; they were orchestrated by the city's unseen hands, each meeting adding another verse to their intertwined destinies. Terry, with his salt-and-pepper hair and piercing blue eyes, saw in Betty a reflection of his own aspirations—a chance to redeem past mistakes and find solace in the arms of someone who understood the price of dreams.

As Betty navigated the contrasting worlds of gritty streets and glamorous venues, she wrestled with the duality of her ambition. Fame glittered like the sequins on her stage costumes, promising a life far removed from the struggles of her youth. Yet, the allure of success came with its own set of challenges—a reality she confronted with every step closer to the spotlight.

The city, with its humid summers and cool winters, mirrored Betty's own journey of highs and lows. It was a place where dreams were born in the shadows and forged under the relentless gaze of fame. Amidst the annual soul music festivals and fashion shows that defined the cultural heartbeat of the city, Betty danced to her own rhythm, each step a defiance of the odds stacked against her.

In the embrace of the city's embrace, Betty found her voice not just as a singer but as a symbol of resilience—a testament to the power of ambition nurtured in the concrete jungle. Her story resonated with those who dared to chase dreams against all odds, weaving a tapestry of passion, desire, and the relentless pursuit of a brighter tomorrow.

Chapter 2 - A Waitress's Song: Dreams on a Platter

BETTY'S DAYS BEGAN much like any other aspiring artist's—juggling trays of steaming plates and dreams on a platter. The diner where she worked, nestled between towering skyscrapers and bustling avenues, was a microcosm of the city's heartbeat. From dawn till dusk, she navigated the ebb and flow of customers, each face a potential listener to her unspoken melodies.

The diner hummed with the rhythm of clinking cutlery and murmured conversations, a symphony of urban life where dreams were both served and savored. Betty, with her apron tied snugly around her waist and a smile that could thaw the frostiest of hearts, was more than a waitress—she was a storyteller in the guise of an everyday server.

Her interactions were vignettes of life in the city: a comforting touch on the shoulder of a weary commuter, a knowing wink shared with a regular patron who secretly nursed dreams of their own. Betty's world was woven from the threads of human connection, each table a stage where stories unfolded over cups of coffee and plates of comfort food.

In the kitchen, amidst the clatter of pots and pans, Betty found solace in the camaraderie of her fellow servers. They were her allies in the daily dance of balancing dreams with reality, their laughter a balm to the bruises left by long shifts and demanding customers. Yet, amidst the chaos, Betty's mind often wandered to the stage where she truly came alive—the smoky clubs where her voice resonated with the soul of the city.

It was there, under the dim glow of stage lights and the haze of cigarette smoke, that Betty shed her waitress persona and became the enchantress of melodies. Her songs were born from the depths of her experiences—the joy of triumphs and the ache of setbacks—all woven into lyrics that echoed the hopes and fears of her listeners.

Terry, ever present in the shadows like a guardian angel cloaked in jazz, often visited the diner on nights when the city seemed to hold its breath. His presence was a reminder of Betty's dual existence—a waitress by day, a songstress by night—a dichotomy that mirrored the city's own contrasting rhythms.

As Betty cleared tables and refilled coffee cups, her mind wandered to the fashion sketches tucked away in a worn leather notebook—a testament to dreams yet to be fully realized. The diner, with its worn linoleum floors and flickering neon sign, became a sanctuary where Betty rehearsed not just her lines but the narrative of her own ascent.

In the heart of the city where dreams were as palpable as the steam rising from freshly brewed coffee, Betty's song was a promise—a melody that dared to defy the odds and soar beyond the confines of her humble beginnings. Each day brought her closer to the precipice of stardom, where the diner's bustling ambiance would be but a distant memory—a chapter in the tale of a waitress who served dreams on a platter.

Betty's journey to the glittering stages of stardom began long before the city's neon lights became her backdrop. It started in the cramped apartment she shared with her grandmother, where the walls echoed with the soulful melodies of old vinyl records and the comforting scent of simmering soul food.

From a young age, Betty's voice was her ticket out of the mundane and into the realm of possibilities. Her grandmother, a beacon of wisdom and resilience, nurtured Betty's talents with gentle encouragement and tough love. Together, they danced in the kitchen to the tunes of Motown legends, their laughter mingling with the strains of music that painted the soundtrack of Betty's childhood.

In those tender years, Betty learned the art of storytelling not just through words but through the cadence of songs that spoke of love lost and dreams found. The apartment, with its peeling wallpaper and creaking floorboards, became a sanctuary where Betty's dreams took flight like notes from a saxophone carried on a summer breeze.

Her grandmother, with hands weathered by years of hard work, sewed costumes for Betty's makeshift performances in the living room-turned-stage. Each stitch was a stitch in the fabric of Betty's ambitions—a testament to the unwavering belief that talent could transcend circumstance.

As Betty grew older, her voice matured like fine wine, resonating with a depth that belied her years. She sang at school talent shows and local community events, her performances imbued with a passion that drew tears from strangers and applause from friends. Yet, it was Terry—the neighborhood's saxophonist with a heart as big as the city itself—who recognized Betty's potential beyond the familiar streets they both called home.

Their chance encounter at a neighborhood block party, where Betty sang amidst the laughter of children and the chatter of neighbors, was a turning point. Terry, leaning against a lamppost with his saxophone cradled like a lover, listened intently as Betty's voice soared above the din of the city.

He saw in Betty the promise of something greater—a star waiting to be born from the ashes of adversity. Terry became Betty's mentor, guiding her through the nuances of performance and the realities of an industry where talent was often overshadowed by the glitz and glamour of superficiality.

Together, they navigated the city's labyrinthine streets, from smoky clubs where dreams mingled with cigarette smoke to studios where Betty's voice was captured on vinyl—a testament to her journey from childhood melodies to the birth of stardom.

In the city where every corner held a story waiting to be told, Betty's rise mirrored the resilience of those who dared to dream against all odds. Her childhood melodies, infused with the wisdom of her grandmother and the passion of her own aspirations, became anthems for a generation searching for truth in the lyrics of life.

As Betty stood on the threshold of stardom, the echoes of her childhood melodies lingered like a whisper in the wind—a reminder of the journey that brought her from humble beginnings to the brink of greatness.

Betty found solace in the rhythm of the city. Each beat pulsated through her veins, echoing the heartbeat of her aspirations. In the urban sprawl where dreams flickered like neon signs, music became her guiding star. It wasn't just the backdrop; it was the essence of her journey from the streets to stardust.

From her small apartment window, Betty could see the city skyline etched against the twilight sky. The distant sounds of jazz mingled with the occasional wail of sirens, painting a tapestry of life in motion. But it was the soulful melodies that spoke to her the loudest. They resonated with her own struggles, offering a soundtrack to her ambitions.

In the heart of the city's nightlife, Betty found herself drawn to smoky clubs where the air was thick with anticipation. Here, under the flickering lights and amidst the sway of bodies, she felt alive. It was in one such club that she first encountered Terry, a saxophonist with a past as turbulent as the notes he played. His music spoke of redemption, of wounds healed by the power of expression.

Terry's saxophone became a bridge between their worlds. Through music, they communicated in a language unspoken yet deeply understood. His melodies wrapped around Betty like a warm embrace, igniting sparks of inspiration that fueled her creative soul. They spent nights lost in improvisation; each note a testament to their shared journey from hardship to hope.

But music wasn't just a passion for Betty; it was a pathway to reinvention. She poured her heart into every lyric she penned, weaving tales of love and resilience into soul-stirring ballads. Her voice, raw and untamed, carried the weight of her experiences, drawing listeners into her world of dreams woven from the threads of reality.

As Betty's fame grew, so did the complexities of her newfound life. The glitz and glamour beckoned, promising a taste of success she had only dreamed of. Yet, beneath the surface, lay the shadows of sacrifices made and the temptations that threatened to derail her journey. Through it all, Terry remained her anchor, his music a constant reminder of the streets they had risen from and the stars they aspired to touch.

In the sultry nights of the city, Betty discovered not only the power of her voice but also the strength of her spirit. Music became more than a muse; it became a mirror reflecting her evolution from a girl with dreams to a woman with a voice that could move mountains.

The city breathed with a rhythm that demanded hustle and grit, a symphony of ambition echoing through its concrete arteries. For Betty, navigating its pulse meant mastering the art of survival while chasing aspirations that shimmered like distant stars.

In the heart of the urban jungle, where neon lights flickered like promises, Betty's days were a whirlwind of motion. From the glamor of photo shoots in penthouse studios to the gritty reality of negotiating contracts in dimly lit offices, she learned the dance of ambition. Each step forward carried the weight of her past, a reminder of the streets that had shaped her resilience.

Yet, amidst the relentless hustle, there were moments of clarity found in unexpected places. On the corner of a bustling street, she encountered Mrs. Jenkins, an elderly woman who sold flowers from a weathered cart. Despite the weariness etched into her features, Mrs. Jenkins greeted each customer with a smile that radiated warmth. Her words, laced with wisdom earned through decades of hardships, resonated with Betty.

"Young lady," Mrs. Jenkins would say, her voice a melody of hope and experience, "Life's a hustle, but don't forget to cherish the beauty in between."

Betty carried those words like a talisman, a reminder to savor the journey amidst the rush towards success. In the maze of ambitions and obligations, she found herself grappling with the dichotomy of staying true to her roots while reaching for the stars. The allure of fame glittered like a mirage, promising validation and recognition beyond her wildest dreams.

Yet, as she climbed higher on the ladder of stardom, Betty confronted the shadows that lurked beneath the spotlight. The pressures of maintaining an image, the relentless scrutiny of public opinion, and the sacrifices demanded by her newfound fame tested her resolve. In the quiet moments before dawn, when the city slept beneath a blanket of stars, she found solace in the memories of simpler times.

It was during one such night that Terry's saxophone called out to her from a dimly lit alley. The haunting melody carried with it echoes of their shared journey, a testament to the dreams they had dared to chase together. In his music, Betty rediscovered the purity of her passion, untainted by the complexities of fame.

As she navigated the labyrinthine corridors of the entertainment industry, Betty learned that survival wasn't just about endurance; it was about preserving the essence of who she was. Her roots became the anchor that steadied her amidst the whirlwind of expectations. From the dusty dance floors of neighborhood clubs to the grand stages that awaited her, she carried with her the spirit of resilience that defined her journey.

In the city's hustle, Betty found not only the trials of ambition but also the triumphs of self-discovery. Each encounter, each setback, and each triumph wove together a tapestry of resilience and aspiration. The streets that had once seemed daunting now pulsed with the heartbeat of possibility, a reminder that amidst the chaos, there existed a path to fulfillment forged by courage and unwavering determination.

Betty stood at the edge of the rooftop, her afro catching the gentle breeze that carried the distant sounds of the city below. It was a night like any other in the urban jungle she called home—a place where dreams flickered like neon lights against the darkness, and every alley whispered stories of both despair and hope.

The night air hung heavy with anticipation as Betty stepped into the spotlight, her heart racing to the rhythm of the music that enveloped her like a warm embrace. This wasn't just another performance; it was a crescendo in the symphony of her dreams—a night where the ordinary met the extraordinary.

Betty had spent countless hours honing her craft, her voice carrying the soulful melodies that had echoed through her grandmother's stories. Tonight, under the glittering lights of the club's stage, she embodied the spirit of perseverance and passion that defined her journey from the tough streets to the threshold of stardom.

Terry watched from the shadows, his gaze unwavering as Betty's voice filled the room, weaving tales of struggle and triumph in the concrete jungle they both called home. For him, music had always been a refuge—a language that transcended the barriers of words, speaking directly to the heart. As Betty sang, he saw not just a performer but kindred spirit whose journey mirrored his own quest for redemption and love.

Their meeting had been serendipitous, orchestrated by the unseen hands of fate that often guided those who dared to dream. Terry had been drawn to Betty's raw talent, recognizing in her the fire that burned within him—a fire tempered by years of navigating the complexities of life on the streets.

As Betty's song reached its crescendo, the audience erupted in applause, their cheers mingling with the beat of Terry's heart. It was a moment frozen in time, where past and present collided in a collision of blaxploitation-inspired narrative, where characters like shaft and foxy brown would feel at home.

In this pulsating cityscape, where every heartbeat was syncopated to the rhythm of ambition and desire, Betty found herself drawn to the allure of fame tempered by the price of success. Her nights were spent crafting fashion sketches that spoke of retro chic and fashion-forward flair, dreams sketched in vibrant colors against the monochrome of everyday struggles.

As Betty and Terry's story unfolded against the backdrop of hot, humid summers and cool, breezy winters, their tale resonated with echoes of historical figures who had paved the way for their dreams. The civil rights movement's echoes reverberated through their journey, reminding them that every step forward was a testament to those who had fought for a chance to shine beneath the neon lights.

Chapter 3 - A Man Among Stars: Charisma in The Shadows

THE CITY SKYLINE GLITTERED with a thousand lights as Terry navigated its streets, a lone figure cloaked in the shadows of towering skyscrapers. For him, the night was both a sanctuary and a battlefield—a stage where charisma and charm danced with danger and deception.

From his days as a young hustler on the streets to his current role as a mentor and community leader, Terry had mastered the art of blending into the background while exuding a magnetic charisma that drew people to him like moths to a flame. His salt-and-pepper hair caught the occasional glint of neon, a reminder of the decades he had spent weaving through the complexities of urban life.

Tonight, however, Terry's thoughts were consumed not by the shadows that lurked in the alleys but by the memory of Betty's rise to stardom. Her voice, once a whisper in the crowded club, had blossomed into a symphony that echoed through the city's soul. It was a testament to her resilience and talent, qualities that Terry admired and sought to nurture in the young dreamers he mentored.

As he walked, Terry passed by familiar landmarks that spoke of a city in constant flux—a metropolis where dreams were born and shattered in equal measure. His own journey from a troubled youth to a pillar of the community had been fraught with challenges, yet each obstacle had forged him into the man he was today: street-wise, charismatic, with a tough exterior hiding a compassionate soul.

In the quiet corners of his mind, Terry wrestled with his fears—fears of losing the people he cared about, fears of failing to protect those he loved. His siblings, estranged and distant, weighed heavily on his heart, their paths diverging long ago in the unforgiving streets they once called home.

Music had always been Terry's solace, his saxophone a conduit for the emotions that words could not express. He played jazz with a fervor that belied his stoic demeanor, each note a testament to the passion that burned within him—a passion tempered by the wisdom of years spent navigating the highs and lows of life.

As Terry approached the community center, he had helped build from the ground up, he saw shadows of young faces peering through its windows, their eyes alight with curiosity and hope. For them, Terry was more than a mentor; he was a beacon of possibility in a world often overshadowed by adversity.

Inside, the walls echoed with laughter and the faint strains of music—a testament to the transformative power of art and community. Terry's journey had come full circle, his past mistakes redeemed through the lives he had touched and the dreams he had helped ignite.

In this chapter of Terry's life, the reader was invited to glimpse the complexities of a man whose charisma shone brightest in the shadows, a man whose journey mirrored the universal quest for purpose and belonging in a city that never slept.

Betty stood at the threshold of a world she had only glimpsed in her wildest dreams. The neon-lit cityscape stretched out before her, a labyrinth of possibilities and pitfalls, where every flicker of light promised both fortune and heartache. From the shadowed alleys where she had grown up, to the glittering stages where stars were born, she felt the pulse of a city that thrived on ambition and desire.

In the heart of this urban jungle, Betty's dreams wove a tapestry of contrasts. Her nights were filled with the soulful melodies that echoed through smoky clubs, where the rhythm of jazz mingled with the heartbeat of the city. Yet, in the daylight, she navigated the concrete realities with a determination forged from years of struggle and sacrifice.

Betty's aspirations soared higher than the skyscrapers that dotted the skyline. With her jet-black hair dancing wild and free, a testament to her untamed spirit, she immersed herself in a world where glamour and grit coalesced. The city became her stage, and every encounter, whether under the glitz of a fashion show or amidst the haze of a crowded club, propelled her closer to her dreams.

Terry, with his salt-and-pepper hair and piercing blue eyes, stood as both mentor and muse in Betty's ascent. His past, etched with shadows of the streets and echoes of old jazz, mirrored her own in ways that transcended mere chance. Together, they navigated the labyrinth of their aspirations, each step forward tempered by the weight of their histories.

From the vibrant nightlife that pulsed with energy to the upscale penthouses where dreams were made tangible, Betty's world expanded with each heartbeat. The sultry summers and cool winters painted a backdrop against which her journey unfolded—a journey that resonated with the cultural tapestry of her heritage, where influences from the civil rights movement and soul music icons intertwined with modern aspirations.

As Betty stood on the precipice of fame, her journey was a symphony of passion and desire, a testament to the allure of success and the price it demanded. Her story, etched against the backdrop of a city that never slept, unfolded with a fashion-forward flair and retro chic that mirrored her own evolution.

In the midst of this urban tapestry, Betty's tale unfolded—a tale of unveiling hidden talents and chasing dreams against all odds. From the depths of her beginnings to the heights of her aspirations, she embodied the spirit of those who dared to defy expectations and carve their names into the annals of history.

Betty's life had always been a dance between the familiar rhythms of her upbringing and the seductive allure of the unknown. Yet, amidst the pulsating heartbeat of the city, fate orchestrated a melody that would intertwine her path with that of a stranger—a harmony of chance encounters and destined moments.

It was on a humid summer evening, the air thick with anticipation and the promise of unexpected turns, that Betty first crossed paths with him. His presence was like a note struck in a jazz composition, drawing her attention with an unspoken familiarity that stirred her soul. In the midst of a crowded club, where the sultry tones of saxophones mingled with laughter and whispered secrets, their eyes met across a room aglow with neon lights.

He was a stranger yet felt oddly familiar, his demeanor a blend of confidence and vulnerability that mirrored her own. In his gaze, Betty glimpsed a reflection of her aspirations and the complexities of her journey—a journey that had woven through the fabric of the city's streets and now stood on the precipice of something profound.

Their encounter was a collision of worlds, where backgrounds faded into insignificance against the backdrop of their shared desires. Betty, with her jet-black hair framing a face that exuded both strength and vulnerability, found herself drawn to his enigmatic aura. He, with a presence that commanded attention yet harbored depths of emotion, sensed in Betty a kindred spirit navigating the same urban labyrinth.

In the tapestry of their unfolding connection, Betty and the stranger—whose name she would later discover as Marcus—found solace amidst the chaos of their respective lives. His journey, like hers, bore the scars of past battles fought in the shadows of the city's towering skyscrapers. From different beginnings yet bound by a common thread of ambition and resilience, they embarked on a tentative dance that echoed the syncopated rhythms of their shared city.

The climate of their burgeoning relationship mirrored the city itself—hot and humid with the promise of cool, breezy moments of respite. As they navigated the complexities of their newfound connection, Betty and Marcus found themselves entwined in a narrative that resonated with the cultural tapestry of their shared heritage. From soulful conversations under the moonlit sky to stolen moments of intimacy amidst the bustling streets, each encounter wove their stories closer together.

In the midst of their burgeoning romance, Betty grappled with fears rooted in her past—of losing independence, of betrayal that lurked in the shadows of her aspirations. Yet, Marcus's presence offered a sanctuary—a refuge where vulnerability became a strength, and trust bloomed like a rare blossom amidst the concrete jungle.

In Marcus, Betty found not only a lover but a muse—an unexpected ally whose presence illuminated the path ahead, where the melody of fate continued to weave their stories together.

In the heart of the city's vibrant nightlife, where every shadow held a promise and every moment shimmered with possibility, Betty and Marcus found themselves swept into a dance of destiny. The air crackled with anticipation as they prepared for a night that would redefine their journey—a night where dreams collided and passions ignited under the watchful gaze of the urban skyline.

Betty, draped in a gown that shimmered like the city lights, felt the weight of anticipation settle around her shoulders. Her jet-black hair cascaded in waves of defiance, a testament to the untamed spirit that had carried her from the streets to the doorstep of fame. Beside her, Marcus stood resplendent in a suit that spoke of old-world charm and contemporary confidence, his presence a beacon amidst the throng of revelers.

As they entered the grand ballroom of one of the city's most storied venues, Betty felt a surge of excitement mingled with trepidation. The room, awash in the glow of crystal chandeliers and the murmur of hushed conversations, seemed to hold its breath in anticipation of their arrival. This night was more than a mere social gathering; it was a testament to their journey—a celebration of resilience and the power of dreams.

Their footsteps echoed on the polished marble floor as they moved in synchrony to the rhythm of a jazz ensemble playing in the corner. The music, a fusion of soulful melodies and sultry undertones, mirrored the complexities of their emotions as they navigated the dance floor. In each other's arms, Betty and Marcus found a sanctuary—a haven where past and future collided in a symphony of desire.

Their conversation, punctuated by laughter and shared confidences, unveiled layers of their respective journeys. Betty spoke of her grandmother's wisdom and the streets that had shaped her resilience. Marcus, in turn, revealed glimpses of a past scarred by loss and a future brightened by newfound hope. In each other's stories, they discovered echoes of their own aspirations—a mutual understanding that transcended words.

As the night unfolded, Betty found herself swept into a whirlwind of emotions—a tapestry of desire and uncertainty that mirrored the city's ever-changing skyline. In Marcus's arms, she glimpsed a future where dreams were within reach—a future where the price of success paled in comparison to the richness of shared moments.

Their dance, reminiscent of the narratives penned by authors like Brenda Jackson, Zane, and Eric Jerome Dickey, unfolded against the backdrop of a city that never slept. Here, amidst the glitz and glamour of high society, Betty and Marcus embodied the essence of their shared journey—a journey marked by resilience, passion, and the unyielding pursuit of dreams.

As the night drew to a close, Betty and Marcus stood on the terrace overlooking the city skyline—a vista that stretched as far as their aspirations. In each other's eyes, they glimpsed the reflection of their own transformation—a testament to the power of love and the dance of destiny that had brought them together.

Chapter 4: The Stage Is Set

BETTY STOOD AT THE edge of the dimly lit stage, bathed in the moonlight that filtered through the open skylight above. Her afro glistened with a touch of stardust, reflecting the city's hustle and dreams. It was here, amidst the rhythmic pulse of jazz and the distant laughter of patrons, that Betty felt most alive.

The nightclub, a cornerstone of the city's nightlife, was Betty's haven. It was where she shed her daytime facade—a waitress in the bustling streets—and stepped into the spotlight, her voice blending effortlessly with the soulful melodies that defined the era. Each note she sang carried the weight of her aspirations, dreams woven into lyrics that spoke of love found and lost, of struggles fought and dreams pursued.

Born into the pulse of the city, Betty had learned early on the dance between survival and ambition. Raised by her grandmother in a neighborhood where hope flickered like a distant star, she had grown up amidst tales of resilience and the promise of a better tomorrow. Her upbringing, though tough, had imbued her with a fierce determination—a determination that now fueled her every performance.

In the audience, amidst the swirling cigarette smoke and the clink of glasses, Terry watched Betty with an intensity that belied his tough exterior. Tall and weathered, his presence commanded respect in the city's streets, where he had once walked a different path. Now, he found solace in the soulful strains of Betty's voice, each song unraveling a piece of his guarded heart.

Betty's journey was more than a quest for fame—it was a testament to the city's heartbeat, where dreams collided with reality under the neon glow. As she sang, her voice echoed through the room, weaving tales of passion and desire, of triumph and loss. Each lyric resonated with the audience—a tapestry of souls seeking solace in the music that bound them together.

Tonight, under the moonlit gaze of the city, Betty's voice soared. It carried with it the echoes of her past and the promise of her future—a future entwined with the stars above and the streets below, where music and moonlight intertwined to create a melody that transcended time

The night air hung heavy with anticipation as Betty stepped out of the nightclub, her heart still racing from the applause that had followed her performance. The city skyline glittered with a thousand lights, each one a testament to dreams realized and ambitions chased. Yet amidst the dazzle, it was Terry's piercing blue eyes that held her attention.

Terry, the enigmatic figure with a past etched in shadows, had become a regular presence in Betty's world. His quiet strength and unwavering support had anchored her as she navigated the highs and lows of her burgeoning career. Their conversations, often punctuated by jazz melodies drifting from nearby cafes, revealed a shared passion for music and a yearning for something deeper.

As they strolled through the quiet streets, Terry spoke of his own journey—a journey scarred by mistakes and tempered by resilience. Betty listened, her admiration for him growing with each word. She saw beyond the tough exterior to the compassionate soul within, a man whose presence stirred emotions she had long kept guarded.

In Terry's company, Betty discovered a new rhythm—a harmony that echoed the ebb and flow of their city's heartbeat. Their interactions, laced with laughter and shared dreams, painted a portrait of a love blossoming amidst the neon-lit backdrop. Yet beneath the surface, doubts lingered—fears born from past betrayals and the precariousness of their respective worlds.

Their bond, like a melody waiting to be composed, unfolded against the backdrop of late-night jam sessions and stolen moments in secluded alleyways. Each encounter deepened their connection, weaving a tapestry of emotions that defied the conventions of their urban reality. Betty found herself drawn to Terry's vulnerability, his fears mirroring her own desire for independence and authenticity.

In the midst of their dance, Terry's saxophone became a symbol of their evolving relationship—a serenade that echoed their unspoken desires and uncharted futures. Together, they navigated the complexities of love in the spotlight, where every glance held the promise of a shared tomorrow and every touch ignited sparks in the dark.

As the city slept and the stars glistened overhead, Betty and Terry stood at the precipice of something extraordinary—a love story written in the language of jazz and illuminated by the city's unyielding glow.

The days melted into weeks, and Betty found herself entwined in a rhythm that defied logic—a melody composed of stolen glances and whispered confessions. In Terry's embrace, she discovered a sanctuary—a place where doubts dissolved into the harmony of their shared passion for music and the city that bound them together.

Their love unfolded like a jazz composition—improvised yet seamless, each note building upon the last to create a symphony of emotions. Terry's presence brought a sense of stability to Betty's whirlwind world, his support unwavering as she navigated the challenges of her burgeoning career. Together, they reveled in the highs—the applause that echoed through crowded clubs—and weathered the lows—the quiet moments when doubts crept in like shadows cast by the moon.

In the intimate corners of the city, Betty and Terry found solace in each other's company. They explored hidden alleys that whispered tales of forgotten dreams, their footsteps echoing against cobblestone streets worn smooth by the passage of time. Beneath the canopy of stars, they shared dreams of a future where love's cadence guided their steps—a future painted in hues of hope and possibility.

Betty's evolution—from a waitress with dreams tucked away in the corners of her heart to a rising star whose voice captivated audiences—mirrored Terry's own transformation. Together, they defied the odds, rewriting the narrative of love in the spotlight. Their bond, forged in the crucible of the city's heartbeat, grew stronger with each passing day—a testament to resilience and the enduring power of passion.

As they navigated the intricacies of their relationship, Betty and Terry discovered the true meaning of harmony. It was not just the blending of melodies or the synchronization of their dreams—it was the understanding that love, like jazz, thrived on spontaneity and shared expression. Their love story, etched against the backdrop of urban vistas and pulsating nightlife, resonated with the soulful melodies that defined their world.

In the quiet moments between performances, Betty often found herself sketching designs—fashion-forward creations that reflected her journey from the streets to the stage. Terry, ever the muse, encouraged her artistic endeavors, his belief in her talents a beacon of light in moments of doubt. Together, they dared to dream beyond the confines of their pasts, embracing a future where love's cadence set the pace for their shared destiny

The night's heavy warmth clung to the city, a blanket of humidity that melded with the pulse of urban beats and neon lights. Betty stood on the edge of the rooftop terrace; the glittering city sprawled beneath her. The heat of the day had given way to a sultry evening, with a gentle breeze that barely stirred her wild afro. She leaned against the railing, lost in the symphony of honking cars, distant laughter, and the soulful hum of a nearby saxophone.

"Betty," a deep, resonant voice called from behind her. She turned to find Terry, his presence as solid and grounding as the city itself. He had a way of appearing from the shadows, his salt-and-pepper hair catching the glow of the city lights. His piercing blue eyes, so rare against his weathered tan, held a mix of sternness and tenderness. He looked like someone who had seen all the city had to offer and carried its secrets with him.

She met his gaze, her own eyes dark and enigmatic, hinting at the dreams and fears swirling beneath her confident exterior. "What are you doing up here, Terry?"

Terry chuckled, a sound as deep and warm as the summer night. "Same thing as you, I suppose. Taking a moment to breathe, to see the city from a different angle." he joined her at the railing, their shoulders almost touching, a silent camaraderie born from shared struggles.

Betty sighed, her breath mingling with the night air. "Sometimes it feels like this city is swallowing me whole. The more I try to make a name for myself, the more it feels like I'm just another face in the crowd."

Terry nodded, understanding her unspoken frustration. "The city has a way of doing that. But remember, it's also a place where dreams are born. You just have to find your voice, your rhythm. And sometimes," he paused,

turning to face her fully, "You need a little guidance to get there."

Betty's eyes sparkled with a mix of curiosity and skepticism. "Guidance? From you?" her tone was teasing, but there was a genuine question beneath her playful facade.

He smiled, a gentle curve that softened his rugged features. "I've been around long enough to know a thing or two. I see potential in you, Betty. More than you might see in yourself right now."

She turned back to the cityscape, biting her lower lip in thought. Terry's words resonated with her. She had always been fiercely independent, a trait honed from years of surviving on the streets and fighting for her place in the world. Accepting help, or even the idea of a mentor, felt foreign and uncomfortable. But there was something about Terry's demeanor – a blend of strength and vulnerability – that made her want to trust him.

"Alright, Terry," she said finally, her voice a mix of resolve and hesitance. "what's the first lesson?"

He leaned on the railing beside her, his eyes scanning the city with the familiarity of someone who had roamed its streets for decades. "The first lesson," he began, "is understanding your worth. In a city like this, people will try to define you by their standards, their rules. You have to learn to define yourself, to stand tall against the pressures and temptations."

Betty frowned, absorbing his words. "Sounds easier said than done."

"It is," Terry agreed. "But you've already taken the hardest step – you're here, willing to listen, willing to learn. That's more than most can say."

They stood in companionable silence, the weight of the city pressing down on them, yet offering a peculiar sense of liberation. The neon lights cast a soft glow over their figures, two souls finding their way through the maze of dreams and desires that was their world. As the moon climbed higher, bathing the city in its silver light, Betty felt a shift within her, a spark of hope and determination kindled by Terry's words.

In that moment, under the moonlit sky, with the city's heartbeat thrumming around them, a new chapter began for Betty. A chapter where mentorship and guidance would illuminate her path, turning the struggles of the concrete jungle into stepping stones towards her stardust dreams.

The nightclub buzzed with anticipation, a throbbing pulse of bass and murmured conversations echoing against the walls adorned with retro posters and glitzy chandeliers. Betty stood backstage, the heavy velvet curtain shielding her from the eager eyes of the audience. Her heart raced in rhythm with the band tuning up, her fingers nervously tracing the sequins on her figure-hugging dress. Tonight was her first big break, a chance to shine not just as a dancer but as a singer.

Terry's voice broke through her reverie. "Ready, kid?" he leaned against the doorway, his broad shoulders filling the frame. The usual cool confidence was evident in his stance, but his eyes held a rare hint of pride and encouragement.

Betty took a deep breath, meeting his gaze. "As ready as I'll ever be." her voice was steady, but the fluttering in her chest betrayed her nerves. She smoothed her dress and adjusted her afro, a cascade of jet-black curls framing her face like a halo.

Terry stepped closer, placing a reassuring hand on her shoulder. "Remember what we talked about. Own that stage. Let them see who you are, what you can do. This is your moment, Betty."

She nodded, the weight of his words grounding her. The countless hours of practice, the late-night sessions under Terry's watchful eye, all led to this. She had come a long way from the streets, and tonight, she would prove that she belonged in the spotlight.

The band started to play a soulful melody, the notes drifting through the air like a promise. The stage manager gave her the signal, and with one last look at Terry, she stepped through the curtain, greeted by a blinding array of lights and the hum of expectation from the crowd.

The nightclub was packed, a sea of faces, some familiar, some not. The stage, a gleaming expanse of polished wood, felt both alien and welcoming under her feet. Betty closed her eyes for a brief moment, letting the music wash over her, the sultry notes of the saxophone intertwining with her heartbeat. She opened her eyes and faced the microphone, the spotlight casting her in a soft glow.

The song began, a haunting ballad that spoke of love lost and found, of dreams deferred but not forgotten. Betty's voice, rich and resonant, filled the room, weaving through the music like a silken thread. Each note, each phrase, carried the weight of her journey, the struggles and triumphs, the heartaches and hopes.

As the first verse ended, the saxophone picked up, and Terry emerged from the shadows, his instrument cradled like a trusted companion. The crowd's murmurs hushed as his soulful playing echoed through the room, a perfect complement to Betty's vocals. Together, they created a tapestry of sound that captivated the audience, a duet that spoke to the heart and soul of everyone present.

Betty's gaze found Terry's across the stage, a silent conversation passing between them. This was more than just a performance; it was a testament to their bond, the mentorship that had blossomed into something profound and transformative. Terry's saxophone sang with a richness that spoke of his own struggles and redemptions, while Betty's voice soared with the promise of a future forged through grit and grace.

The audience was enraptured, swaying to the music, their faces alight with admiration and wonder. In that moment, Betty felt a surge of confidence, a clarity that she had never known before. She belonged here, under the bright lights, sharing her talent with the world. This stage was not just a platform but a testament to her journey from the gritty alleyways to the glitz and glamor of the nightlife.

As the song drew to a close, the final notes hanging in the air like a lover's whisper, the crowd erupted into applause, a thunderous wave that washed over Betty and Terry. She turned to him, a smile spreading across her face, her eyes sparkling with unshed tears of joy and gratitude. Terry nodded, his own eyes reflecting a deep sense of pride and accomplishment.

They took a bow together, the applause swelling around them, a symphony of approval and appreciation. For Betty, this was not just a performance, but a declaration of her dreams and a celebration of the mentorship that had guided her here. As they left the stage, the lingering strains of their duet echoed in her heart, a reminder that she was no longer alone in her quest for stardom. Together, they had created something beautiful, a testament to the power of dreams and the bonds that help shape them.

Chapter 5 - Bonds In the Beat: Melodies of The Soul

THE MORNING AFTER THEIR performance, the city awoke to a sweltering heat that shimmered over the rooftops and pressed against the alleyways. Betty's tiny apartment, a cozy space adorned with mismatched furniture and colorful fabrics, was a sanctuary away from the chaos of the streets below. She sat by the window, the sunlight streaming in and casting warm patterns on her smooth brown skin, her wild afro catching the light like a halo of shadows and golden highlights.

Terry's saxophone rested on her cluttered coffee table, a silent witness to the previous night's triumph. Betty picked it up gently, feeling the cool metal against her fingers. She marveled at how something so inanimate could produce music that spoke to the very core of her being.

A knock on the door interrupted her reverie. She placed the saxophone back on the table and opened the door to find Terry standing there, his usual calm demeanor softened by a hint of a smile. He held two cups of coffee, the rich aroma wafting through the small hallway.

"thought you might need this," he said, offering her a cup. His salt-and-pepper hair was slightly tousled, and his eyes, a piercing blue, carried a warmth that contrasted with his rugged exterior.

Betty accepted the coffee, their fingers brushing briefly. "Thanks, Terry." she stepped aside to let him in, closing the door behind him. "Did you get any sleep?" he chuckled, setting his own cup down on the table. "Enough. How about you? Still riding the high from last night?" she nodded, taking a sip of her coffee. "It was incredible. I never imagined... Well, you know. The crowd, the energy. It was like a dream."

Terry sat on the worn-out sofa, watching her with a mixture of pride and amusement. "You were fantastic, Betty. But it's just the beginning.

You've got the talent, now you need to keep pushing, keep creating. The music isn't just a performance; it's a connection. It's about reaching people, touching their souls."

Betty joined him on the sofa, her eyes drifting to the saxophone. "You always talk about music like it's a living thing. Like it has a soul of its own."

"It does," Terry replied, his voice low and earnest. "Music is a reflection of our experiences, our emotions. It's the bond that connects us, no matter where we come from or what we've been through."

She looked at him, really looked at him, and saw the man beneath the tough exterior. A man who had faced his own demons, who had found solace in the melodies he created. "Is that why you play?" she asked softly. "To connect?"

Terry nodded, his gaze distant for a moment. "When I play, it's like speaking without words. The music says what I can't. It's a way to heal, to communicate. And when you sing, Betty, you do the same thing. You have a gift, a voice that can reach people in ways they might not even realize."

His words lingered in the air, filling the small room with a sense of understanding and camaraderie. Betty felt a swell of emotion, a recognition of the bond they shared through their music. It was more than just notes and rhythms; it was a melding of their souls, an expression of their deepest selves.

"I want to keep doing this," Betty said, her voice determined. "I want to make music that matters, that makes people feel something. But I don't want to do it alone."

Terry's smile widened, his eyes crinkling at the corners. "You won't be alone. We'll do it together. We'll find that beat, that melody that speaks to people. We'll create something beautiful, something real."

The rest of the morning passed in a blur of melodies and laughter, their voices mingling with the music that flowed from Terry's saxophone and Betty's rich, soulful singing. The apartment, with its modest decor and vibrant fabrics, became a haven for their creativity, a place where their bond through music blossomed into something profound and enduring.

As the day wore on and the sun climbed higher, Betty felt a sense of contentment and purpose. She and Terry were more than just a performer and a mentor; they were partners in a journey that transcended the stage. Their music, born from the struggles and triumphs of their lives, was a testament to the power of connection and the melodies of the soul.

The city's nightlife had begun to stir, casting long shadows and a cascade of lights across the apartment's cramped interior. Betty and Terry sat across from each other at her small kitchen table, the remnants of their impromptu dinner—a hodgepodge of takeout containers and mismatched cutlery—scattered between them. The room was filled with the faint strains of soul music from a nearby radio, a familiar comfort that softened the evening's edges.

Betty traced a pattern on the tablecloth with her finger, her mind drifting over the events of the past weeks. Their musical journey together had brought them closer, intertwining their lives in ways she hadn't anticipated. She glanced up at Terry, his rugged features softened in the dim light, his eyes reflecting a calm intensity as he sipped his coffee.

"Terry," she began, her voice hesitant. "Have you ever thought about what comes next? I mean, after all of this?" her gesture encompassed the room, their music, their partnership.

He set his mug down, the faint clink a punctuation in the soft silence. "You mean beyond the music?" he asked, his eyes meeting hers with an openness that was rare for him.

"Yeah," she said, leaning back in her chair. "I mean, I've been so focused on getting to this point, on finding my voice and making a name for myself. But now, I'm starting to wonder... What does the future hold? For both of us?"

Terry smiled, a slow, thoughtful expression that creased the corners of his eyes. "I've been thinking about that too. It's like we're standing at the edge of something new, something unknown. And it's exciting, but it's also... Uncertain."

Betty nodded, her heart quickening. The uncertainty of the future had always been a source of anxiety for her, a shadow that loomed over her dreams. But with Terry, that uncertainty seemed less daunting, more like a blank canvas waiting to be filled with the colors of their combined talents and ambitions.

She looked down, gathering her thoughts. "I guess what I'm trying to say is... I don't just see you as my mentor anymore, Terry. You're more than that to me. You've become a part of my life, my dreams. And I want to know what that means for us."

The vulnerability in her voice was palpable, a fragile thread stretched between them. Terry reached across the table, his rough, calloused hand enveloping hers. The warmth of his touch was reassuring, grounding her in the present moment.

"Betty," he said softly, his gaze unwavering. "you're not the only one who's been thinking about the future. What we have—it's special. It's not just about the music anymore. It's about us, about what we can build together."

Her breath caught at his words, a surge of emotion flooding through her. "So... What are you saying?" she whispered, her eyes searching his.

Terry squeezed her hand gently. "I'm saying that I want to be part of your future, Betty. Not just as a mentor, but as someone who cares about you, who believes in you. I want us to face whatever comes next together." The confession hung in the air, a delicate promise of what could be. Betty felt a warmth spread through her chest, a sense of clarity and connection that dispelled the shadows of doubt and fear. She smiled, a radiant expression that lit up her features, her eyes shimmering with unshed tears.

"I want that too," she said, her voice firm with conviction. "I want us to face the future together. Whatever it brings."

Their hands remained intertwined on the table, a silent affirmation of their shared commitment. The night outside continued to hum with life, but within the walls of Betty's apartment, a new sense of possibility bloomed. The music on the radio shifted to a slow, soulful ballad, the lyrics speaking of love and hope, of dreams whispered in the quiet moments between dusk and dawn.

As the evening deepened, Betty and Terry found themselves drawn together by the unspoken bond they had forged, a connection that transcended the roles of mentor and protégé. It was a bond built on shared dreams and mutual respect, on the melodies they created and the affection that had quietly grown between them.

They sat together, their future unfolding in the tender echoes of their conversation, in the promises whispered in the soft light of the evening. It was a beginning, a whisper of tomorrow that held the promise of something beautiful and enduring, something that would carry them forward into whatever lay ahead.

The city pulsed with its own rhythm as night fell, the air thick with humidity and the scent of sizzling street food mingling with the aroma of exhaust fumes. Betty and Terry walked side by side through the bustling streets, their conversation weaving through the noise of traffic and the distant strains of live music spilling from open doorways. The city, with its vibrant nightlife and chaotic energy, felt like a living entity, a backdrop to their burgeoning connection.

They reached a small jazz club nestled between towering buildings, its neon sign flickering intermittently. The club was a haven of retro charm, its walls adorned with vintage album covers and photographs of music legends. Inside, the dim lighting and intimate setting created a cocoon of sound and emotion, a perfect stage for the night's performance.

Betty glanced at Terry, her heart pounding with anticipation and a hint of anxiety. They were here to perform again, but tonight felt different. Their recent conversations had added a new layer to their relationship, a complexity that both thrilled and unnerved her. As they settled into a corner booth, she couldn't shake the feeling that tonight would be a turning point, not just for their music, but for them.

The band began to play, a smooth, soulful tune that wrapped around the audience like a warm embrace. Terry's saxophone sat beside him, its polished surface catching the light.

He turned to Betty, his expression a mix of determination and tenderness. "Ready?" he asked, his voice barely audible over the music.

She nodded, her confidence bolstered by his steady presence. They took the stage together, the crowd's murmurs fading as the first notes filled the room. The music was a conversation between their instruments and their voices, a dialogue of longing and connection, of dreams shared and conflicts simmering beneath the surface.

As they performed, Betty felt the weight of their unspoken emotions pressing against the lyrics she sang, each word a reflection of the bond that had grown between them. The audience was captivated, their eyes fixed on the duo as if they were witnessing something rare and beautiful. But beneath the surface, Betty sensed a tension, a conflict that had yet to be resolved.

After their set, they returned to their booth, the applause still ringing in their ears. Betty's gaze drifted to Terry, who was lost in thought, his fingers absently tracing the rim of his glass. She could feel the distance between them, a gap that had widened despite their closeness.

"Terry," she said softly, reaching out to touch his hand. "what's on your mind?" He looked up, his eyes shadowed with an emotion she couldn't quite decipher. "Betty, I've been thinking about what we talked about. About us. And I... I have some doubts."

her heart skipped a beat, the words striking like a discordant note in their symphony. "Doubts? About what?" she asked, her voice tinged with uncertainty.

He sighed, his gaze dropping to their intertwined hands. "About whether we can balance this—our music, our personal lives. I've been down this road before, and it's not easy. It's hard to keep things separate, to avoid letting one affect the other."

Betty's chest tightened. She had feared this moment, the clash between their professional aspirations and their personal feelings. "I know it's complicated," she said, trying to keep her voice steady. "But I believe we can make it work. We've come so far together, Terry. We can't just walk away from what we have."

He shook his head, a pained expression crossing his features. "I'm not saying we should walk away. I just... I don't want to risk everything we've built. Our music, our partnership—it means too much to me."

His words hung in the air, a fragile truth that cut through the night's warmth. Betty felt a surge of frustration and fear, the certainty she had felt earlier slipping away. "But what about us, Terry? What about what we've started? Don't we owe it to ourselves to try?"

Terry met her gaze, his blue eyes filled with a mixture of longing and doubt. "We do. But I'm afraid, Betty. Afraid of losing what we have. Of letting our emotions get in the way of our dreams."

Betty's heart ached at his confession, a mirror to her own fears. She squeezed his hand, her grip firm with determination. "We can't let fear hold us back, Terry. We've faced so much already. We can't let this be the thing that stops us." he nodded slowly, his gaze softening. "you're right," he murmured. "We can't let fear win. But we need to be careful. We need to make sure that we don't let our personal feelings derail our music." they sat in silence, the sounds of the city outside mingling with the lingering echoes of their performance. The conflict between their dreams and their affection was a delicate balance, a dance they would have to navigate with care.

As they left the club, the cool night air a welcome contrast to the heat inside, Betty felt a sense of resolve. Their path would not be easy, but she was willing to fight for it, to find a harmony between their music and their growing love. The city lights stretched before them, a symphony of possibilities waiting to be explored. Together, they would face the challenges, finding strength in their bond and the melodies they created, whispering promises of a future where love and ambition could coexist.

Chapter 6 - Rivals In the Shadows: The Dance of Competitors

THE GRITTY, VIBRANT heart of the city's entertainment district was alive with energy, neon signs flickering above dimly lit alleys and the pulsating beats of music seeping from clubs and bars. Betty and Terry navigated through the throng of revelers, their hands loosely intertwined, a subtle affirmation of their connection amid the chaos. Tonight, they were heading to a new club, the enclave, a place rumored to be a hotspot for emerging talent and fierce competition.

The enclave was a stark contrast to the other venues they had performed in—its sleek, modern exterior and the sophisticated crowd setting it apart from the usual smoky, retro joints they frequented. The club's interior was a blend of cutting-edge design and classic elegance, with dark wood panels, soft leather booths, and a stage framed by shimmering curtains. The audience, a mix of hipsters and music aficionados, buzzed with anticipation for the night's showcase—a talent contest that promised not just fame, but the coveted spotlight in the city's elite music circles.

As they entered, Betty felt a shiver of excitement tinged with apprehension. This was more than just another gig; it was a stage where reputations could be made or broken, where rivals lurked in the shadows, ready to pounce at any sign of weakness. She tightened her grip on Terry's hand, drawing strength from his reassuring presence.

They found a table near the back, the perfect vantage point to observe the competitors. Terry, ever the strategist, scanned the room with a keen eye, his street-smart instincts alert to the nuances of the crowd and the performers. Betty followed his gaze, her own nerves thrumming with a mix of anxiety and determination.

"Keep your focus," Terry murmured, leaning closer. "There's a lot of talent here, but remember why we're doing this. Show them what you've got."

Betty nodded, her resolve hardening. She had come too far to be intimidated now. The lights dimmed, and the first performer took the stage—a sultry jazz singer whose voice wrapped around the audience like velvet. The room erupted in applause, the bar set high from the outset.

As the night progressed, each act brought a new flavor to the competition—an electrifying guitarist, a poet whose words flowed like liquid gold, a dance troupe that moved with a precision that was almost hypnotic. Betty's heart pounded in her chest, a drumbeat of anticipation as her turn approached. She couldn't help but notice a particular performer, a rival she had faced before in smaller venues—a striking woman with a powerful voice and a presence that demanded attention. She went by the name Angelique, and her performance was a masterclass in control and charisma, her gaze challenging Betty from across the room.

When Angelique finished, the applause was thunderous, the audience clearly captivated by her magnetic stage presence. Betty's pulse quickened, the sense of competition sharpening her focus. She glanced at Terry, his expression a mask of calm confidence. "You've got this, Betty," he said, his voice low and steady. "Just be yourself. They'll see your light."

Taking a deep breath, Betty made her way to the stage. The spotlight was blinding, the audience a sea of faces blurred by nerves and the intensity of the moment. The band struck up a tune, a soulful melody that she had chosen carefully for its ability to showcase her range and emotional depth. As she began to sing, her voice filled the space, rich and resonant, each note carrying the weight of her journey, the struggles and triumphs that had shaped her.

The audience fell silent, their attention riveted by her performance. Betty's eyes scanned the crowd, finding angelique's gaze fixed on her, a mixture of respect and rivalry in her eyes. It was a silent acknowledgment of the competition between them, a dance of talents where only one could claim the night's victory.

Betty's voice soared, her emotions pouring into the lyrics, a testament to her passion and dedication. She could feel the energy in the room shift, the crowd leaning in, captivated by the raw power of her performance. The final note hung in the air like a promise, a declaration of her place on this stage, in this world of fierce competitors and glittering dreams.

The applause was deafening, a wave of approval that washed over her, filling her with a sense of accomplishment and exhilaration. She took a bow, her eyes finding Terry's in the dim light, his smile a beacon of pride and support.

As she left the stage, angelique approached, her expression inscrutable. "That was impressive," she said, her voice smooth and measured. "you've got talent, Betty. But this isn't over. I'll see you on the next stage."

Betty nodded, a smile playing on her lips. "I wouldn't expect anything less. May the best woman win."

Angelique's lips curved into a knowing smirk before she turned and melted into the crowd. Betty watched her go, the thrill of the competition igniting a fire within her. She rejoined Terry, who wrapped an arm around her shoulders, pulling her close. "You were amazing," he said softly, his voice filled with admiration.

She leaned into him, the tension of the night easing into a warm glow of satisfaction. "Thanks, Terry. I couldn't have done it without you."

As they left the enclave, the city's lights stretching before them like a shimmering promise, Betty felt a surge of confidence and determination. The competition had only just begun, and she was ready to face whatever came next, with Terry by her side and her dreams burning bright in the neon-lit shadows.

The sudden rush of stardom was intoxicating—a whirlwind of adoring fans, glittering lights, and high-profile performances that seemed to sweep Betty off her feet and into a dazzling new world. In just a few short weeks after their triumphant night at the enclave, Betty's name was on everyone's lips. She had become the darling of the city's music scene, her voice hailed as the next big thing in soul and jazz.

The transformation was almost surreal. Betty went from small gigs in smoky clubs to headlining at prestigious venues, her face splashed across magazine covers and billboards. Invitations to exclusive parties and offers from record labels flooded in, each promising her the world. She was no longer just a hopeful talent; she was a star on the rise, her presence commanding attention wherever she went.

But with the bright lights came shadows—long and dark, cast by the relentless pursuit of fame and the demands that came with it. The pressure to constantly deliver, to be perfect in the public eye, began to weigh heavily on Betty's shoulders. The endless cycle of rehearsals, interviews, and performances left little room for anything else, her days blurring into a frenetic pace that left her exhausted and isolated.

The once-cozy apartment that had been her sanctuary now felt more like a distant memory. Betty had moved into a sleek, upscale condo in the heart of the city, a place befitting her new status but devoid of the warmth and familiarity of her old life. The spacious rooms, with their designer furnishings and panoramic views, felt cold and impersonal, a stark contrast to the vibrancy of her past.

Late at night, Betty would sit by the floor-to-ceiling windows, gazing out at the cityscape, the twinkling lights a reminder of how far she had come—and how far she felt from the person she used to be. The phone calls with Terry had become sporadic, their conversations strained by the distance and the demands of her career. The bond they had forged, once so strong and unbreakable, seemed to be fraying at the edges, worn thin by the harsh realities of her newfound fame.

One evening, after a particularly grueling rehearsal, Betty found herself alone in her condo, the silence oppressive. She had just returned from a meeting with her manager, who had laid out the schedule for her upcoming tour—a grueling circuit that promised to elevate her career even further, but at the cost of her already dwindling personal time. She felt a pang of loneliness, a yearning for the simplicity and authenticity of her earlier days.

Her phone buzzed, interrupting her thoughts. It was a message from Terry: "Hey, just checking in. Haven't heard from you in a while. How's everything going?"

Betty stared at the screen, a wave of guilt washing over her. She hadn't meant to drift apart from Terry, but the demands of fame had created a chasm between them that seemed to grow wider with each passing day. She typed a quick response, her fingers hesitating over the keys: "Hey Terry. It's been crazy. Miss you. Let's catch up soon?"

His reply came almost immediately: "I miss you too, Betty. Let's talk tonight?".

Her heart ached at the simple, heartfelt message. She agreed, her mind racing as she tried to find a quiet space amidst the noise and expectations of her new life. When she finally called him later that evening, his voice was a balm to her frayed nerves, a reminder of the stability and support he had always offered.

"Betty," he said gently, his tone filled with concern. "You sound tired. Are you okay?"

"I'm... I'm managing," she replied, her voice barely above a whisper. "it's just a lot, Terry. The shows, the press... It's all so overwhelming. Sometimes I feel like I'm losing myself in all of this."

Terry sighed, the sound a mix of empathy and frustration. "I wish I could be there with you, to help you through this. You don't have to do it alone, you know."

"I know," she said, tears pricking at her eyes. "I just... I don't know how to balance everything. I wanted this so badly, but now that I have it, it feels like it's slipping through my fingers."

"There's a price to fame," Terry said softly. "But it shouldn't cost you your happiness or your peace of mind. Remember why you started this journey, Betty. It wasn't just for the applause or the headlines. It was for the music, for the joy it brings you."

His words resonated deep within her, a stark reminder of the passion that had fueled her dreams from the start. She took a deep breath, trying to center herself amidst the chaos. "you're right, Terry. I need to find that joy again. I need to find a way to hold onto who I am, even in all of this."

They talked late into the night, the conversation a much-needed anchor in the storm of her life. As the call ended, Betty felt a renewed sense of clarity and resolve. She knew that the road ahead would not be easy, that the pressures of fame would continue to test her, but she was determined to stay true to herself and the love for music that had brought her this far.

In the days that followed, Betty made a conscious effort to reclaim her sense of self amidst the whirlwind of her career. She carved out time for quiet reflection, for reconnecting with the things that brought her joy beyond the stage. She reached out to old friends, re-establishing bonds that fame had threatened to sever, and made plans to spend more time with Terry, valuing the connection that had become a lifeline in her turbulent world.

As she navigated the lonely road of stardom, Betty learned to embrace the balance between the allure of the spotlight and the need for personal fulfillment. The city lights continued to shine, but now they seemed less like a distant, overwhelming force and more like guiding stars, leading her toward a future where fame and happiness could coexist, a symphony of love and ambition playing in harmony.

the city was cloaked in night, its streets washed in the glow of flickering neon and the distant hum of traffic. From the expansive balcony of her condo, Betty gazed at the skyline, a glass of wine in hand, the chill of the evening air biting through her thin silk robe. The city, usually a source of inspiration and energy, now felt like a distant, indifferent giant, its ceaseless motion only amplifying the stillness and unease that settled over her.

Inside, the condo was an elegant fortress of solitude, its stylish decor and cutting-edge amenities a stark contrast to the turmoil roiling within Betty. The accolades, the bright lights, the endless cycle of performances and public appearances had created a facade of success, yet beneath the surface, doubts had begun to fester, creeping into the shadows of her mind.

Betty took a sip of her wine, the liquid a bitter balm against the knot of anxiety tightening in her chest. The events of the past weeks played out in her thoughts like a fractured melody—glittering success marred by moments of uncertainty and self-doubt. Her rise to fame had been meteoric; yet with each step higher, the ground beneath her seemed less stable, the stakes higher, the pressures more crushing.

She turned away from the cityscape, her reflection in the floor-to-ceiling windows a haunting image of confidence and fragility. The familiar ache of fear clawed at her, a reminder of the precarious balance she was trying to maintain between her public persona and her private struggles. The fear that had once driven her to excel now felt like a relentless echo, amplifying her insecurities, casting long shadows over her every move.

Betty set her glass down and wandered into the living room, the silence of the condo amplifying the disquiet in her mind. Her phone buzzed with a new message, the screen lighting up with Terry's name. She hesitated, a pang of guilt twisting in her stomach. Their conversations had become strained, their once-unbreakable bond now strained under the weight of her career and the distance it had created.

"Hey Betty. Been thinking about you. How are you holding up?" the message was simple, filled with concern and care, a stark reminder of the support she had been unintentionally distancing herself from.

Her fingers hovered over the keyboard, her thoughts a tangled mess of longing and apprehension. How could she explain the depths of her fear and doubt, the relentless pressure that threatened to erode the very essence of who she was? She typed and deleted several responses, each one feeling inadequate, before finally settling on a brief reply: "It's been tough, Terry. Can we talk?"

his response was almost immediate, a lifeline thrown across the chasm that had grown between them: "Of course. Call me when you're ready."

Taking a deep breath, Betty dialed his number, the familiar sound of his voice a soothing balm against the storm of her emotions. "Terry," she said, her voice barely above a whisper. "I don't know if I can do this anymore. The pressure, the expectations... It's all too much."

"Talk to me, Betty," he urged gently. "What's going on? You've never let anything stop you before. What's different now?"

"It's everything," she confessed, the words spilling out in a rush. "The spotlight, the constant scrutiny... I feel like I'm losing myself in all of this. I don't even know who I am anymore, or if I'm enough to handle it all."

Terry's silence was a palpable presence, a space for her to release the fears that had been suffocating her. "You're more than enough, Betty," he said finally, his voice a steady anchor in her turmoil. "But you're right. Fame can be a heavy burden. It's okay to feel scared. It's okay to have doubts. What's important is not letting them define you."

His words struck a chord deep within her, a reminder of the resilience and determination that had fueled her journey from the start. "I just... I don't want to let everyone down," she admitted, her voice breaking. "I've worked so hard to get here, but I'm afraid of failing, of not living up to everyone's expectations."

"You won't let anyone down," Terry assured her. "But you have to remember why you started this journey in the first place. It wasn't for the fame or the accolades. It was for the love of music, for the joy it brings you. Don't lose sight of that."

Betty closed her eyes, his words a comforting echo in the dark. "you're right," she murmured. "I need to reconnect with that, with what made me fall in love with music in the first place. I've been so caught up in trying to meet everyone's expectations that I've forgotten why I'm here."

As their conversation continued, Betty felt the tight knot of fear and doubt begin to loosen, replaced by a tentative sense of clarity and resolve. Terry's unwavering support and understanding were a beacon of light in the shadows that had engulfed her, a reminder that she wasn't alone in her struggle.

After they said their goodbyes, Betty sat in the stillness of her living room, a renewed sense of purpose slowly unfurling within her. She knew that the road ahead would be fraught with challenges and moments of doubt, but she was determined to face them with the same courage and passion that had brought her this far. The fears that had threatened to overwhelm her would not be her downfall; instead, they would become the stepping stones to a deeper understanding of herself and her music.

The city outside continued its relentless hum, but Betty felt a new sense of calm amidst the chaos. She rose, crossing to the grand piano that stood by the window, its polished surface reflecting the city lights. Sitting down, she let her fingers drift over the keys, the familiar touch grounding her in the present, reconnecting her with the essence of her talent and passion. The first notes of a new melody filled the room, a quiet testament to her resolve and the unbroken thread of her dreams.

The early morning light filtered through the gauzy curtains of Betty's bedroom, casting a gentle glow on the chaos that had become her life. She lay awake, staring at the ceiling, the events of the past days replaying in her mind like a discordant symphony. The betrayal by Leo had left her raw, her trust shattered, yet she had emerged from the confrontation with a newfound determination to reclaim her destiny.

But the trials of her professional life were not the only challenges she faced. The echoes of her conflict with Leo had reverberated through her personal life, straining the bonds with those she cared about most. The relationship with Terry, her steadfast supporter and confidant, had been her anchor in the tumultuous sea of fame. Yet, as she rose from the bed and padded to the kitchen to brew her morning coffee, Betty couldn't shake the feeling that even this bond was under siege, tested by the relentless demands of her career and the shadows of her past.

The rich aroma of freshly brewed coffee filled the air, a small comfort in the swirling uncertainty. Betty wrapped her hands around the warm mug, seeking solace in its heat as she sat by the window, gazing out at the bustling city below. The condo, a testament to her success, now felt like a gilded cage, each luxurious detail a reminder of the price she had paid for her dreams. The ache of doubt and fear lingered, a constant companion that whispered of impending failure and loneliness.

Her phone buzzed, shattering the morning quiet. It was a message from Terry: "We need to talk. Meet me at the jazz spot tonight?"

the jazz spot—where they had first met, their connection forged over the soulful strains of a saxophone and the shared dream of rising above their struggles. The thought of revisiting that place, now tinged with the bittersweet memories of their journey together, filled her with a mix of anticipation and apprehension. Betty took a deep breath and replied, "I'll be there at 7."

The day passed in a blur of rehearsals and meetings, her focus fractured by the impending conversation with Terry. By the time evening rolled around, Betty was a bundle of nerves, her mind racing with a thousand unspoken questions and fears. She arrived at the jazz spot just as the sun dipped below the horizon, the familiar neon sign flickering in the twilight.

The club was dimly lit, the intimate atmosphere alive with the soft hum of conversations and the gentle strains of a live jazz band. Terry was already there, seated at a secluded corner table, his expression unreadable as he nursed a glass of whiskey. Betty approached him, her heart pounding with the weight of their unspoken words.

"Terry," she greeted him softly, sliding into the seat opposite him. "Thanks for meeting me."

He looked up, his blue eyes filled with a mixture of concern and something deeper, more complicated. "Betty," he said, his voice steady but tinged with an edge of tension. "We need to talk about what's been going on."

She nodded, her throat tight. "I know. Everything's been... Overwhelming."

Terry took a deep breath, his gaze unwavering. "I've been watching you struggle, Betty. The pressure, the betrayal by Leo—it's taking a toll on you. And it's affecting us. I've tried to be there for you, but it feels like you're slipping away, lost in the whirlwind of your career."

The truth of his words hit her like a punch to the gut, the reality of their strained relationship stark and undeniable. "I'm sorry, Terry," she whispered, her voice breaking. "I didn't mean to shut you out. I've just been so caught up in everything, trying to navigate this crazy world on my own."

"I know," he said gently, reaching across the table to take her hand. "But you don't have to do it alone. I'm here, and I want to be here for you. But you have to let me in, Betty. You have to trust me, even when things get tough."

His touch was warm, grounding her amidst the swirling doubts and fears. Betty's eyes filled with tears, the weight of her emotions threatening to overwhelm her. "I do trust you, Terry," she said, her voice trembling. "I'm just scared. Scared of failing, of losing myself, of losing you."

Terry's grip on her hand tightened, his expression softening. "You won't lose me," he promised. "But we need to face these challenges together. Fame is a lonely road if you try to walk it alone. I love you, Betty. But we have to be a team, even in the face of all this chaos."

The simple, heartfelt declaration pierced through the fog of her doubts, a beacon of hope amidst the turmoil. Betty squeezed his hand, the warmth of his presence a balm to her frayed nerves. "I love you too,

Terry," she confessed, the words a fragile thread of honesty. "And I don't want to lose what we have. I'm willing to fight for us, for this."

Terry's eyes held hers, his gaze unwavering. "Then we fight together," he said firmly. "We face the trials, the betrayals, the pressures—everything. But we do it side by side, as partners."

A tentative smile tugged at Betty's lips, the first genuine smile she had felt in days. "Together," she agreed, the word a promise and a prayer. "We'll face it all together."

The band struck up a slow, soulful tune, the music weaving through the air like a promise of better days. Betty and Terry sat there, hands intertwined, the silent understanding between them a balm to the wounds of the past. The trials of fame and the betrayals of trust had tested their bond, but the strength of their love and commitment had emerged resilient, a testament to their shared journey and the harmony of their hearts.

As the night deepened, Betty felt a renewed sense of hope, the chords of her life slowly mending into a harmonious melody. The road ahead would be challenging, filled with trials and tribulations, but with Terry by her side, she felt ready to face whatever came next. Together, they would navigate the symphony of love and life, their hearts in harmony amidst the trials that lay ahead.

Betty stood backstage, her heart pounding in sync with the distant bass line thumping through the walls. Tonight was different; the air crackled with anticipation, a palpable energy that mirrored her own nerves. The spotlight beckoned like a distant promise, yet it carried the weight of every dream she had dared to cradle in her chest.

In the urban jungle of the city, where concrete reigned and neon lights whispered promises of stardom, Betty's journey had been etched in the alleys and streets she once called home. From a childhood framed by the gentle but firm love of her grandmother to the nights spent singing in smoky clubs, she had woven her story with threads of resilience and unyielding ambition.

Her afro, a wild crown atop her deep brown complexion, caught the dim backstage lights in a halo of defiance. Betty's gaze, mysterious and dark, held the secrets of a thousand melodies she had sung and a thousand dreams she had yet to chase down. Tonight, those dreams hovered tantalizingly close, just beyond the velvet curtains.

Across the stage, Terry paced with the confident grace of a man who knew both the harsh rhythms of the streets and the soulful melodies of redemption. His salt-and-pepper hair spoke of wisdom hard-earned, his eyes—piercing blue—betrayed the turmoil of a past he could not outrun. Yet, in Betty's eyes, he was more than his scars; he was a beacon of possibility, a melody waiting to be harmonized with her own.

The music swelled, a cascade of jazz notes that wrapped around them both like a lover's embrace. Betty stepped into the spotlight, her voice weaving through the smoky air, each note a testament to the struggles she had known and the triumphs she had tasted. Terry watched from the wings, his heart in his throat, as Betty's performance unfolded like a tapestry of passion and desire, woven from threads of ambition and soulful yearning.

As she sang, the audience became not just spectators but witnesses to a story unfolding—one of resilience and revelation, of dreams deferred but never abandoned. The stage became a sanctuary where Betty shed the weight of doubt and fear, where her voice soared like a phoenix rising from the ashes of forgotten promises.

In that fleeting moment, under the glare of the spotlight, Betty and Terry's eyes met—a silent exchange that spoke volumes. It was a recognition of shared dreams and unspoken fears, of the dance between ambition and the allure of fame. In that embrace of music and emotion, they found not just a stage but a canvas upon which their stories intertwined, painted with the hues of passion and determination.

The applause thundered like a storm, breaking the spell cast by Betty's voice. Terry stepped forward; his hand outstretched. Betty hesitated for a heartbeat, then took it, feeling the rough calluses of his fingers against her own. Together, they stood under the neon lights, amid the glitz and glamor that adorned their city. It was a moment suspended in time, where pasts were redeemed and futures rewritten—one soulful note at a time.

Chapter 7 - Melodies Of Longing: Hearts Entwined

BETTY HAD ALWAYS BELIEVED in the power of music to bridge the gaps between hearts, but that night on the stage with Terry, she discovered its ability to intertwine souls. In the days that followed their electrifying performance, their paths seemed destined to converge with a cadence that mirrored the beats of their own hearts.

Amid the urban backdrop of their bustling city, where summer heat gave way to cool breezes that whispered secrets of the night, Betty and Terry found themselves drawn to each other like notes harmonizing in a jazz composition. Their encounters were fleeting at first—a shared glance across a crowded street, a chance meeting in a dimly lit jazz club where Terry's saxophone whispered secrets of longing and regret.

Betty, with her jet-black afro framing a face that exuded both strength and vulnerability, found solace in Terry's presence. His salt-and-pepper hair, cropped close against the world's harshness, held stories she longed to unravel. Each conversation, laden with the weight of unspoken dreams and shared aspirations, revealed layers of their souls that resonated with a haunting familiarity.

They walked the city's streets together, their footsteps echoing against the concrete as they navigated the labyrinth of their intertwined pasts. Betty spoke of her grandmother's unwavering love and the dreams she had woven from the fabric of their modest home. Terry shared glimpses of a turbulent youth marked by wrong turns and hard lessons, tempered by the tender embrace of his aging mother.

In the sultry nights, when the city shimmered under the glow of streetlights and neon signs, they found themselves entangled in conversations that spanned the spectrum of human experience—love, loss, hope, and the elusive promise of redemption. Betty's fears of losing her independence melted in Terry's reassuring presence, his fears of failing those he loved soothed by her unwavering belief in second chances.

Their romance unfolded not in grand gestures but in stolen moments and whispered confidences shared under the starlit sky. Terry's hands, weathered from years of holding onto fleeting dreams, found solace in Betty's touch, her fingers tracing the lines of resilience etched into his skin. Together, they navigated the delicate dance of trust and vulnerability, forging a bond that defied the boundaries of time and circumstance.

In the heart of the city, where soulful melodies echoed through the bustling streets and hidden alleyways, Betty and Terry discovered that their dreams, once deferred, could find new life in each other's embrace. Their love story became a testament to the transformative power of music and the enduring strength found in the quiet spaces between notes—a melody of longing that resonated far beyond the stage where it had first been born.

As they stood together under the canopy of stars, their hearts entwined like lyrics to a cherished song, Betty knew that with Terry by her side, she had found not just a partner but a muse who inspired her to reach for the stars once more.

in the pulse of the city's nightlife, where the beat of jazz and the rhythm of desire intertwined, Betty and Terry found themselves swept into a dance that transcended mere steps. Their romance, kindled amidst the backdrop of smoky clubs and starlit evenings, blossomed into a symphony of passion and longing—a dance where every touch spoke of unspoken desires and whispered promises.

Betty's days became a kaleidoscope of rehearsals and fittings, as she chased her dreams of becoming more than just a voice in the night.

Terry, ever the guardian of her aspirations, stood by her side with a quiet strength that belied the storms he had weathered. His saxophone wove melodies that echoed through their shared moments, a soundtrack to their burgeoning love affair.

In the dim corners of jazz clubs, where the air was thick with the scent of bourbon and the murmurs of patrons lost in their own reveries, Betty and Terry found refuge in each other's arms. Their conversations lingered over glasses of whiskey, where words danced between them like fireflies in the summer dusk—illuminating fears, hopes, and the undeniable pull of their mutual attraction.

Their first kiss, stolen beneath the glow of a streetlamp that flickered like a hesitant heart, ignited a firestorm of emotions that neither could deny. Betty's lips, soft against Terry's weathered skin, tasted of dreams fulfilled and promises yet to be made. His embrace, strong and sure, anchored her to a reality where love was not just a fleeting melody but a symphony of two souls finding harmony.

As they explored the depths of their passion, each touch became a revelation—an exploration of boundaries pushed and inhibitions shed. In Terry's arms, Betty discovered a freedom she had never dared to imagine, a liberation from the constraints of her past and the uncertainties of her future. His hands, calloused yet tender, traced the contours of her dreams as though sculpting them into reality.

Amidst the backdrop of a city that never slept, where the neon lights painted their silhouettes against the concrete canvas, Betty and Terry danced the dance of desire. Their bodies moved in syncopated rhythms, choreographed by the ebb and flow of their shared yearning. In those stolen moments, they found solace from the cacophony of life's demands, weaving a tapestry of intimacy that defied the boundaries of time and place.

But beneath the heady euphoria of newfound love, shadows lurked in the corners of their hearts. Betty's fears of losing her independence resurfaced like distant echoes, tempered only by Terry's steadfast presence. His own insecurities, rooted in a past haunted by mistakes and regrets, threatened to cast a pall over their burgeoning romance.

Yet, in the warmth of their embrace and the promise of shared tomorrows, Betty and Terry discovered that love was not just a fleeting emotion but a commitment forged in the crucible of their shared journey. Their dance of desire unfolded not as a mere interlude but as a testament to the transformative power of love—the kind that burned bright against the backdrop of life's darkest moments.

As they surrendered to the pull of passion's embrace, Betty and Terry knew that their love story was more than just a chapter in their lives—it was the melody that would guide them through the symphony of their shared future.

Betty stood in front of the mirror, her fingers gently tracing the intricate lines of her latest fashion sketch. Each curve and angle told a story—a narrative of resilience and elegance woven together in fabric. Her afro, wild and free, framed a face that reflected both determination and vulnerability. Tonight, she was debuting her designs at a small but prestigious fashion show, a pivotal moment in her journey from the streets to stardust.

The venue buzzed with anticipation, the air thick with the scent of ambition and dreams. Betty's heart raced as she watched models glide down the runway in her creations, each piece a testament to her creativity and unwavering spirit. Among the crowd, she caught glimpses of Terry, his salt-and-pepper hair a stark contrast against the neon lights that adorned the stage.

Terry had been her anchor through turbulent waters, his steady presence and belief in her talents a constant source of strength. As she navigated the glamorous but unforgiving world of entertainment, Terry remained her rock—a reminder of where she came from and the heights she could reach. Their bond, forged in the crucible of shared dreams and past struggles, grew deeper with each passing day.

The music swelled, a soulful melody that echoed through the venue, setting hearts alight with passion and desire. Betty's eyes met Terry's across the room, a silent exchange that spoke volumes—a promise of unwavering support and unspoken love. In that fleeting moment, amidst the glitz and glamor, Betty realized that true success wasn't just measured in accolades or fame; it was found in the embrace of those who saw her for who she truly was.

As the last model disappeared behind the curtain, applause erupted like thunder, reverberating off the walls of the penthouse venue. Betty stepped forward, her hand intertwined with Terry's, their fingers entwined in a silent vow to chase dreams against all odds. Together, they stood, two souls bound by a shared journey of struggle and triumph in the concrete jungle, their hearts beating in rhythm to the symphony of touch—notes of love that transcended time and place.

The night air hung heavy with anticipation as Betty stood on the balcony of Terry's penthouse, overlooking the city sprawled below. Neon lights flickered in the distance, casting a kaleidoscope of colors on the streets below—a stark contrast to the quiet intimacy of their sanctuary in the sky. The events of the fashion show lingered in her mind, but tonight, there was a tension in the air—a whisper of secrets waiting to be unveiled.

Terry stood beside her, his gaze fixed on the horizon, his saxophone resting against the railing. The jazz notes from earlier still echoed in Betty's ears, a soulful soundtrack to the evening's unfolding drama. She turned to him, searching his weathered face for clues, for the answers that had eluded her for so long.

"Tell me, Terry," Betty began, her voice barely above a whisper, "About your past. About the shadows you've carried."

Terry's eyes, usually warm and inviting, turned distant—a flicker of hesitation before he spoke. "I grew up rough, Betty. On the streets where every day was a battle. I did things—things I'm not proud of." his voice cracked with emotion, the weight of his words hanging heavy in the night air.

Betty reached out, her hand finding his, fingers interlacing in a silent show of solidarity. "You don't have to carry those burdens alone," she murmured, her voice a balm against the wounds of his past. "We all have shadows, Terry. But together, we can face them."

Silence enveloped them like a cocoon, broken only by the distant sounds of the city below—a reminder of the world outside their private haven. Terry turned to Betty, his eyes searching hers for understanding, for acceptance. In that moment, beneath the canopy of stars and the soft glow of the moon, they forged a bond stronger than any secret, deeper than any darkness.

"I've done things too, Terry," Betty confessed, her voice steady despite the turmoil within. "Things that haunt me. But tonight, let's lay them bare. Let's embrace the truth, whatever it may be." and so, against the backdrop of a city alive with dreams and desires, Betty and Terry faced their truths—unveiling hidden talents and chasing dreams against all odds. In each other's arms, they found solace, a sanctuary from the whispers of the night and the secrets that threatened to tear them apart.

As the first rays of dawn painted the sky in hues of pink and gold, Betty knew that their journey was far from over. Together, they would navigate the twists and turns of their intertwined destinies, their hearts beating in rhythm to the symphony of life—a melody of love, loss, and the courage to embrace it all.

In the days that followed their heartfelt revelations, Betty and Terry found themselves immersed in a newfound closeness—a harmony that resonated in every glance, every touch. The city embraced them with its vibrant energy, a backdrop to their evolving story of love and ambition intertwined.

Betty threw herself into her fashion designs with renewed vigor, each sketch infused with a passion born of newfound clarity. Terry, ever the supportive muse, played his saxophone on lazy afternoons, the soulful notes weaving tales of their journey from the streets to stardust. Together, they painted a canvas of hope against the backdrop of a city that never slept.

Amidst the hustle and bustle of their respective worlds—Betty navigating the glitz and glamor of the fashion scene, Terry mentoring young talents in the community—they carved out moments of quiet intimacy. On lazy Sunday mornings, they shared breakfast on the balcony, the city unfolding beneath them like a promise of endless possibilities.

But beneath the veneer of newfound happiness, shadows stirred—a reminder that their pasts were not easily shaken. Betty's rise in the fashion world brought newfound attention, both admiration and envy casting long shadows. Terry's past, though veiled in secrecy, occasionally resurfaced in whispers that threatened to unravel their fragile peace.

One evening, as they strolled through the soul music festival, Betty sensed Terry's unease—a tension in his shoulders, a distance in his gaze. She stopped, her hand gently finding his, fingers intertwining in a silent plea for reassurance.

"Terry, what's wrong?" Betty asked softly, her heart tightening with worry. "you've been distant lately. Is it... The past?"

Terry sighed, his gaze turning inward as he struggled to find the words. "Betty, I've been trying to protect you—from who I was, from the mistakes I've made. But I can't erase the past."

Betty squeezed his hand gently, her eyes searching his for understanding. "Terry, you don't have to face it alone. We face it together, remember?"

Terry nodded slowly, a mixture of gratitude and apprehension in his expression. "I want to believe that, Betty. I do."

as the music swirled around them, a crescendo of emotions filled the air—love, fear, and the courage to confront their vulnerabilities. In each other's arms, they found solace once more, their hearts beating in sync with the symphony of their shared journey.

Love's crescendo echoed through the night, a melody of resilience and hope that transcended the challenges ahead. Betty and Terry stood together, ready to face whatever harmonies life composed for them, their love a testament to the beauty of embracing both the light and the shadows.

The city skyline glowed with the promise of a new day as Betty and Terry stood hand in hand on the rooftop terrace of Terry's penthouse. The air was crisp with the onset of autumn, a gentle breeze carrying the scent of change and possibility. Beneath them, the city stirred awake, its heartbeat synchronized with theirs—a testament to the resilience of dreams and the power of love's resolution.

Betty leaned against the railing, her gaze fixed on the horizon where the sun slowly peeked above the skyscrapers. Terry stood beside her, his presence a comforting anchor amidst the swirling emotions that had defined their journey from strangers to soulmates.

"We've come a long way, haven't we?" Betty whispered, her voice soft with a mix of wonder and gratitude.

Terry turned to her, his eyes reflecting the morning light as he nodded. "Yes, we have. And we've faced our share of challenges."

Betty smiled, a flicker of determination in her eyes. "But we faced them together. That's what matters." As they stood in companionable silence, memories of their shared moments flooded their minds—the exhilaration of Betty's fashion successes, the quiet nights of music and whispered confessions, and the undeniable strength they drew from each other's presence.

"I've been thinking," Terry began, his voice hesitant yet resolute. "About us, about our future."

Betty turned to him, her heart skipping a beat at the earnestness in his tone. "What about our future, Terry?"

Terry took a deep breath, his hand reaching into his pocket. "I want us to build something together, Betty. Something that's ours, something that speaks of who we are."

he withdrew a small velvet box, its contents catching the first rays of dawn—a glimmering testament to his hopes and dreams. Betty's breath caught in her throat as Terry knelt before her, his eyes locked with hers in a moment that transcended words.

"Betty," Terry began, his voice steady despite the weight of his emotions. "Will you marry me?"

tears welled up in Betty's eyes, her heart overflowing with love and joy. "Yes, Terry. Yes, a thousand times yes."

In that fleeting moment, against the backdrop of a city alive with possibilities, Betty and Terry found their harmonies in harmony—a symphony of love's resolution that echoed through the years to come. As they embraced, their laughter mingling with the city's morning chorus, they knew that their journey was far from over.

Hand in hand, they walked into the sunrise, ready to face the melodies of life together—undaunted, unstoppable, and forever bound by the timeless rhythm of their love.

www.ingramcontent.com/pod-product-compliance
Lightning Source LLC
LaVergne TN
LVHW091230150826
845673LV00003B/1086

* 9 7 9 8 2 3 0 0 3 4 6 2 9 *